Robin Hill School

Butterfly Garden

written by Margaret McNamara
illustrated by Mike Gordon

Ready-to-Read

Simon Spotlight

New York   London   Toronto   Sydney   New Delhi

For Natalie and her friends
at Burgundy Farm School—M. M.

Simon Spotlight
An imprint of Simon & Schuster Children's Publishing Division
1230 Avenue of the Americas, New York, NY 10020
Text copyright © 2012 by Margaret McNamara
Illustrations copyright © 2012 by Mike Gordon
For information about special discounts for bulk purchases, please contact
Simon & Schuster Special Sales at 1-866-506-1949 or business@simonandschuster.com.
The Simon & Schuster Speakers Bureau can bring authors to your live event. For more
information or to book an event contact the Simon & Schuster Speakers Bureau at
1-866-248-3049 or visit our website at www.simonspeakers.com.
Manufactured in the United States 0212 LAK
2 4 6 8 10 9 7 5 3 1
Library of Congress Cataloging-in-Publication Data
McNamara, Margaret.
Butterfly garden / by Margaret McNamara ; illustrated by Mike Gordon. — 1st ed.
p. cm. — (Robin Hill School)
Summary: Mrs. Connor's first-graders watch as caterpillars
slowly turn into butterflies in the butterfly garden at Robin Hill School.
ISBN 978-1-4424-3642-8 (pbk. : alk. paper)
ISBN 978-1-4424-3643-5 (hardcover : alk. paper)
ISBN 978-1-4424-3644-2 (e-book)
[1. Metamorphosis—Fiction. 2. Caterpillars—Fiction. 3. Butterflies—Fiction.
4. Schools—Fiction.] I. Gordon, Mike, 1948 Mar. 16- ill. II. Title.
PZ7.M47879343Bu 2012 [E]—dc23 2011027167

Mrs. Connor held up
a package.
"Who can guess what
is in here?" she asked.

The first graders
did not know.

"I will give you a hint,"
said Mrs. Connor.

"It is something that changes from one thing to another."

"Is it a monster?"

asked Eigen.

"Is it a superhero?"

asked Michael.

"It is not a monster
or a superhero,"
said Mrs. Connor.

She opened the package
carefully.
Inside, there were
five tiny bugs.

"Caterpillars!"
yelled the first graders.

"We are going to learn about butterflies," said Mrs. Connor.

"Then why are we looking
at caterpillars?" asked Emma.

"Caterpillars turn into butterflies," said Hannah. "This shows how they do it," said Mrs. Connor.

LIFE CYCLE OF THE BUTTERFLY

Egg

Caterpillar

Chrysalis

Butterfly

At first the caterpillars
did not move much.
"Are they asleep?"
asked Katie.

"Are they dead?"
asked Jamie.
"No," said Mrs. Connor.
"They are working
hard."

After a few days

they got bigger . . .

and bigger . . .

and bigger!

After a week the caterpillars climbed to the top of the jar.

"They are hanging

upside down!" said Katie.

The next day Mrs. Connor said, "Look! They covered themselves up so they can grow wings."

Mrs. Connor moved them carefully into the butterfly garden.

The first graders waited
for eleven more days.
"They are getting darker!"
said Eigen.

On the twelfth day,
Mrs. Connor said,
"Class! Come quickly!"

The whole class gathered
around the butterfly garden.
"Look!" said Nick.

"Something is coming out!"
said Nia.

"It is a butterfly!"
said Eigen.

The butterflies carefully
opened up their wings.
"Why are they so small?"
asked Emma.

"They will get bigger very soon," said Mrs. Connor.

When the class came back from recess, there were three butterflies in the garden.

All their wings were big
and beautiful.

When they were all big
enough, the class let
them go.
"That was even better
than a superhero,"
said Michael.